Let's Explore the Jungle

This Book Belongs To: _____

Meet "Tommy" the Tiger.
Tommy walks through the forest all alone.
Tommy lost his family long ago.
Tommy is lonely.

As Tommy is walking he comes across an elephant.
The elephant is all by herself.
The elephant looks sad.
Tommy goes over to say hello to the elephant.

Tommy introduces himself.
"Hi," he says, "I'm Tommy the Tiger."
The elephant looks down and says,
"Hi. I'm Eden, the Elephant."

Tommy asks Eden, "Why are you crying?"
Eden says, "I lost my family, and I miss them so much."
Tommy says, "I lost my family long ago too,"
"I walk the forest alone, but it would be nice to walk with you."

Eden agreed, and smiled for the first time.
So they started to walk together.
They walked and talked about life before they met one another.
They became very close friends, and watched after each other daily.

One day while walking, they came across a river with a waterfall.
Eden noticed that on one side of the river,
there was a family of ducks.
Tommy noticed in the river there was a duck
floating toward the waterfall in a panic.
Tommy told Eden that they had to try to save the duck.

Eden could wade in the water without going under due to her size.
Tommy rode on her back as they moved closer to the duck.
The water was flowing heavy, but Tommy was brave.
Tommy picked up the duck from the water
and they made it to the other side of the river safe.

The duck said, "Thank you so much for saving me."
"My name is Dempsey the Duck."
Eden and Tommy introduced themselves to Dempsey too,
and both said,
"You're welcome."

The flocks of ducks that Eden had noticed earlier
were gone from the riverside.
Dempsey had been left all alone.
Dempsey said,
"I wandered off by myself, slipped in the water, and can't swim very
well. They didn't even know that I was gone."
She bowed her head, and thought that she would be alone forever.

Eden and Tommy looked at each other.
They knew they couldn't leave Dempsey alone.
Eden offered for Dempsey to travel with them.
Tommy said,
"We walk the forest, and look after one another,
we can do the same for you."

Dempsey was overjoyed that she wouldn't have to be alone.
They all walked through the forest together.
Dempsey hoped that she would one day see her family again,
But felt happy because she knew she at least had Tommy and Eden
that cared for her.

Eden, Tommy, and Dempsey walked through the forest together
as a family.
They slept together, ate together, and laughed together day after day.
They made sure that each other were safe.
They grew love and respect for one another.

One day as they were walking through the forest,
Eden heard a noise in the tree tops.
Tommy told Dempsey to get behind him until he knew it was safe.
Eden spotted a monkey tangled in the tree branches above them.

The monkey was moving
but appeared to be stuck in some tree limbs and branches.
He was making a lot of noise.
Eden tried to call out to the monkey to calm down.
He noticed the three of them down below and stopped making noise.

Tommy asked the monkey if he needed some help.
The monkey, not sure if the tiger would hurt him,
didn't speak, but kept moving.
Eden asked if he needed some help.
The monkey, not sure if the elephant would take his food,
didn't speak, but kept moving.

Finally, Dempsey asked if Eden could lift
her up closer to the monkey.
Eden lifted her up, and Dempsey asked,
"Can I help you get untangled from this tree?"
The monkey felt safer with Dempsey,
and shook his head in agreement.

Dempsey used her beak to cut the tree branches
to help the monkey break free.
The monkey initially started jumping from tree to tree
so happy to be free again.
He realized he didn't thank the duck,
so he went back to say,
"Thanks!"

Dempsey introduced herself,
"Hi, I'm Dempsey the duck. You're welcome."
The monkey introduced himself,
"Hey, I'm Max the Monkey."

Dempsey introduced Max to Eden and Tommy.
She wanted to assure Max that it was safe to talk to them too.
They all began to talk about their journey together so far.
Max was touched by their stories.

It was getting late
and Eden wanted to get everyone to safe spaces for sleeping.
She asked Max about his family and home.
Max stated that he takes care of himself now.
Eden invited Max to join them. Max agreed.

Days and nights passed.
Eden had taken on a motherly role.
Tommy had the fatherly role.
Dempsey was the younger sister, and
Max was the older brother.

Despite their differences,
They grew to be a blended family.
They loved one another, and took care of one another.

They shared new adventures together, every day...

"The Jungle Family"

Reading Comprehension Questions:

Pre-K - Kindergarten Questions:

1. What does the cover tell you about the book?

2. Can you name the four characters in the book?

3. What was your favorite part of the book? Why?

1st Grade Questions:

1. If you could be one of the character's in the book, who would you be and why?

2. If your family was in the story, what character would each member be and why?

3. Name two problems that are encountered in the story.

2nd Grade Questions:

1. Is the book fiction or nonfiction, and how do you know?

2. Name one problem in the story that happened, and how it was solved. Would you solve it differently, and how?

3. What did you learn from the book?

3rd Grade Questions:

1. Why do you think Tommy asked Eden to walk the jungle with him?

2. What do you wonder about after reading this story?

3. If you could ask any character a question in the story, what character and what question would you ask?

Please visit **colanidesigns.com** for Jungle Family clothing and accessories

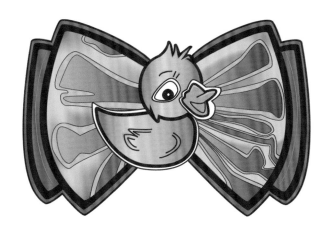

CREATE YOUR OWN BOW TIE

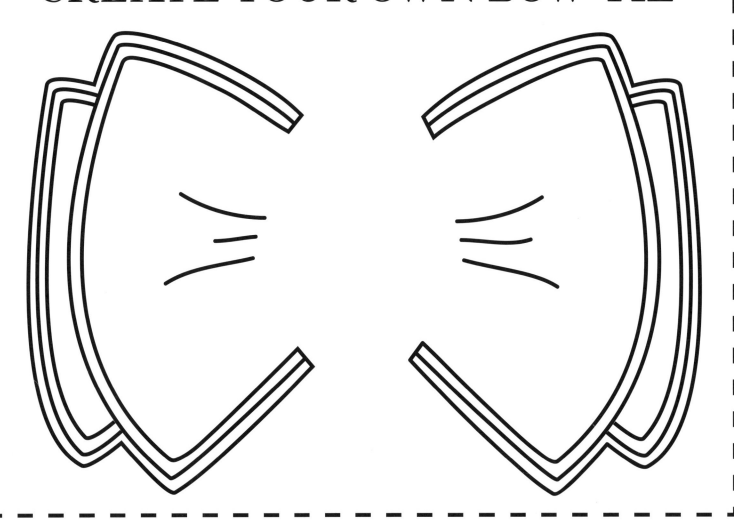

CREATE YOUR OWN
JUNGLE FAMILY

I AM

I AM STRONG
I AM LOVED
I AM SMART
I AM COURAGEOUS
I AM THE JUNGLE FAMILY

TERELLE COLEY

About The Authors

Terelle Coley has always had a passion for fashion and working with children. After obtaining a Bachelor's and a Master's degree he realized that he also wanted to be a business owner. Serving as an art teacher and an advocate for children for several years, he has used his art ability to help many children display their creativity and talents. Since starting Colani, now known as Colani Designs, he has geared his business toward making children's books and children's apparel unique. His future plans are to continue to make designs for children that educates them about dealing with life situations, the importance of family, and understanding the importance of given and receiving love.

Demetria Dove Nickens is an advocate for children and has a passion for finding ways to teach disadvantaged children to realize their dreams and develop paths to reach them. Being a Big Sister with the Big Brothers/Big Sisters Program, and having a Master's degree in Counseling Psychology with a specialization in Child & Adolescent Psychology has helped her to pursue her passion of helping children. Her most recent accomplishment and newest love, is her greatest yet, becoming a mother of a son. She feels blessed to be given this honor, and will continue to share her passion with her child and other children that need her talents.